This book is dedicated to kind and courageous children everywhere.

A Note for Parents and Teachers:

Like all ***Short Vowel Adventures****,* **Cubs in a Tub** *highlights one short vowel sound, in this case the short "u" sound. We believe this phonics focus helps beginning readers gain skill and confidence. After the story, we've included two* ***Story Starters*** *just for fun.* ***Story Starters*** *are open-ended questions that can be used as a jumping-off place for conversation, storytelling, and imaginative writing.*

At BraveMouse Books we believe the most important part of any reading program is the shared experience of a good story. We hope you'll enjoy **Cubs in a Tub** *with a child you love!*

The BraveMouse Team

Cubs in a Tub

by Molly Coxe

BraveMouse Readers

Gus is glum.
Russ is glum.
"Ho hum."
"Ho hum."

"Let's have some fun,"
says Gus.

“What’s up?” says Mum.
“Not much,” says Gus.

“Tug!” says Gus.
“I am tugging!” says Russ.

“Run!” says Russ.
“I am running!” says Gus.

"Cowabunga!"
say Gus and Russ.

“Hi, Muff! Hi, Fluff!”
says Gus.

"Bye, Muff! Bye, Fluff!"
says Russ.

“Uh oh.”

Jumps!

Bumps!

Lumps!

“My tum!” says Russ.
“My bum!” says Gus.

"Is that Mum?"
says Russ.

“Mum!”

Mum tugs the tub
up, up, up.

“One more run?” says Mum.
“Yes!” says Russ.
“Look! Hunny wants to come!”

“Cowabunga!”
say Gus, Russ, Hunny, and Mum.

Story Starters

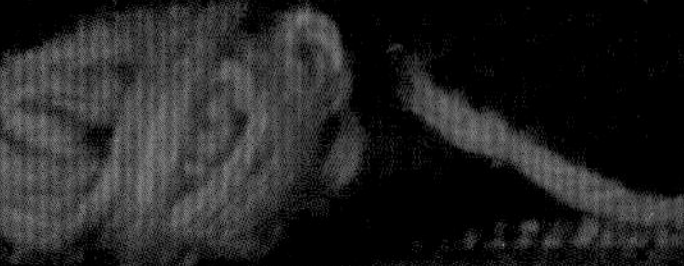

Mum is humming.
What is she humming?

Muff and Fluff
are stuck in the mud.
What will Muff and Fluff do?